MW01124818

Michelle is a Pittsburgh, PA native whose journey as an author began with writing professional technical and marketing documents as a chemical engineer. As part of her son's bedtime routine, she began telling him stories about the things he loves. She then started writing these stories down as children's books so that others can enjoy them too.

Michelle's stories transport young readers into new worlds, full of color, humor, and fantasy with relatable characters. In each story, she focuses on values and critical thinking that will help her son and other young readers learn and develop new skills.

Michelle D'Amico

Harvey's Hamburgers

AUSTIN MACAULEY PUBLISHERS™
LONDON • CAMBRIDGE • NEW YORK • SHARJAH

Copyright © Michelle D'Amico 2024

Ordering Information
Quantity sales: Special discounts are available on quantity purchases by corporations, associations, and others. For details, contact the publisher at the address below.

Publisher's Cataloging-in-Publication data
D'Amico, Michelle
Harvey's Hamburgers

ISBN 9781685626785 (Paperback)
ISBN 9781685626792 (Hardback)
ISBN 9798886930320 (ePub e-book)

Library of Congress Control Number: 2024912043

www.austinmacauley.com/us

First Published 2024
Austin Macauley Publishers LLC
40 Wall Street, 33rd Floor, Suite 3302
New York, NY 10005
USA

mail-usa@austinmacauley.com
+1 (646) 5125767

For Liam.

Harvey the Iguanodon was quite peculiar compared to the other dinosaurs in his herd. While most of his friends were green with a bit of yellow, Harvey stood out. He was bright orange with purple stripes. Harvey loved being different. He was proud of his amazing colors.

Most of Harvey's friends were farmers, tending to their crops with the rest of the herd. But Harvey loved to explore the valley and try new things. One of his favorite things to do was to cook. He didn't get a lot of practice though, as most Iguanodons were happy to munch on leaves, and they didn't need cooking for that. Still, Harvey was happy to cook for himself.

6

The other Iguanodons ate every kind of leaf you can imagine from broad palm fronds to little pine needles. They liked cycads and flowers most of all. Harvey ate plants as well, but he also tried every other kind of food that he could find. He had one food that was his very favorite. Harvey LOVED hamburgers!

Harvey would eat a hamburger every day if he could. He decided one day that he wanted to share his love of hamburgers with his herd and the other dinosaurs who lived in the valley. So, he started a food truck.

The food truck was decorated just like Harvey himself. It was orange with purple stripes and had a GIANT sign that read *Harvey's Hamburgers*. Harvey was very proud of his food truck, and he was excited to serve his delicious hamburgers to the other dinosaurs.

He prepared his ingredients, opened up the service window, and got ready for business. Harvey waited for customers. He saw a few of his Iguanodon friends coming along the path.

"Welcome to Harvey's Hamburgers," he bellowed as they got closer.

"Hamburgers?" they said. "Yuck! Don't you have any 'normal' food?" And they continued walking past without trying Harvey's hamburgers.

A group of Diplodocus soon came along, and the same thing happened. Then a Stegosaurus, more Iguanodons, and a group of Triceratops walked past the food truck without stopping. Harvey began to worry.

What if no one wants to try my hamburgers?
He closed up his truck for that day without selling a single hamburger.

The next day, Harvey tried again. He prepared his ingredients, opened up the windows, and got ready for business. Some of his family members stopped by.

"Harvey, this will never work," they told him. "No Iguanodons will ever eat a hamburger when they have delicious vegetables available. Just come back home and work with us on the farm." But Harvey wouldn't give up on his dream.

Harvey continued to offer hamburgers to every dinosaur he saw. And each one turned him down. Then he saw them! An Allosaurus and Carnotaurus coming down the path.

Oh no! Predators! thought Harvey. He slammed the food truck's window shut and dove under the table.

Knock. Knock. Harvey trembled in fear. He heard them just outside the truck.

"Hello? Is anyone here?" called out the Allosaurus. "We would love some hamburgers."

Hamburgers? They want hamburgers? Harvey thought to himself.

Harvey was still scared, but he cracked open the service window and peeked out. "You really want hamburgers? You're not going to eat me?" Harvey asked them.

16

"Eat you? No way! Why would we eat you when we can have hamburgers!" the Carnotaurus told him. "We would like five each please."

Harvey's eyes got very wide. "Ten hamburgers. Coming right up!" He got to work, and soon delicious smells began to waft through the valley. Harvey served them, and the Carnotaurus and Allosaurus devoured their food with glee. "These were delicious!" they told Harvey. "We'll be back soon."

Harvey was thrilled to have made a sale, even if carnivores made him nervous. And soon the delicious cooking smells began to draw in other dinosaurs.

He saw a Megalosaurus and Dilophosaurus walking towards him. Once again, he slammed the window shut and dove under the table.

Knock. Knock. Harvey quaked in fear as he heard them outside.

"Hello?" asked the Megalosaurus. "Is anyone here? We would love some hamburgers."

They want hamburgers too, he thought to himself.

Harvey was still scared, but he was a little braver this time. He cracked open the service window.

20

"How many hamburgers would you like?" Harvey asked them. "We would like seven each please." Harvey's eyes got very, very wide.

"Fourteen burgers. Coming right up!" He got to work. Harvey served them, and the Megalosaurus and Dilophosaurus devoured the burgers.
"These were delicious!" they told Harvey. "We will be back soon."

22

What a day! Harvey thought. *It was a surprising day but a good day.*

Harvey cleaned up and went to bed. He wasn't sure how he felt about predator dinosaurs being his best customers, especially when his own family and friends wouldn't even try his food. But he was proud of his hard work, and he decided then to cook for whoever wanted to come to Harvey's Hamburgers.

The next day, he had hardly had a chance to prepare his ingredients when he heard the knocking start. Harvey opened the window and jumped back in shock. He had a line, a huge line, a huge line full of HUGE dinosaurs! First up were the dinosaurs from yesterday, but the line stretched further than Harvey could see.

"We told a few friends," the Allosaurus told Harvey. "We hope you don't mind."

Harvey got to work. Five for the Allosaurus, five for the Carnotaurus, seven each for the Dilophosaurus and Megalosaurus, fifteen for the Tyrannosaurus Rex. Harvey almost ran when she stepped up to the window. Eight for the Velociraptor family, eleven for the Spinosaurus. And on it went all day long. Harvey barely had a chance to cook one order before another dinosaur stepped up.

By the end of the day, he was exhausted. He went to bed with a smile on his face. It was another surprising and good day.

The next day, Harvey did his preparations and opened the window. But this time, he wasn't surprised by the line. He thought that yesterday was busy! Harvey served dinosaur after dinosaur.

He saw a few of his Iguanodon friends start towards the truck at one point and then turn and run away when they saw who was in line for his food. But Harvey was too busy to care. He was thrilled that dinosaurs were enjoying his cooking.

By the end of the day, he was exhausted, but he went to bed with a smile on his face.

Harvey now knew what would happen when he woke up. So, he prepared his truck as fast as he could.

"Welcome to Harvey's Hamburgers!" he cried out as he opened the window. As the day wore on, a few of his friends tried to get close to see what was happening.

"Are you going to get in line?" a Giganotosaurus asked Harvey's friends.
"Get in line?" one Iguanodon asked. "Why would we do that?"

"To try the best hamburger in the valley, of course!" the Giganotosaurus replied, shaking his head.

32

One brave Iguanodon stepped into line. He was sure he would be eaten by one of the predators and started shaking. But the other dinosaurs were too busy talking about Harvey's hamburgers to pay any attention to him. The Giganotosaurus put in his order (thirty-seven burgers!) and then the Iguanodon stepped up. Harvey was shocked to see one of his herd at the truck.

"Welcome!" he said. "What would you like to order?"

"A hamburger, I guess," the Iguanodon whispered. Harvey served it up, and his friend took a bite. "It's pretty yummy." he said. But before Harvey could respond, the Iguanodon saw a Tyrannosaurus Rex heading this way and ran for it.

34

Harvey's friend told everybody in the valley about Harvey and his hamburgers. And the following day, Harvey's line was filled with his usual customers. But he also saw a few nervous Iguanodons in between a Rugops and Torvosaurus, a brave Diplodocus right next to a Majungasaurus, and a little Parasaurolophus trying to ignore the excited Compsognathus jumping with excitement behind her.

Harvey was delighted. All he ever wanted was to share his love of food and cooking with his friends in the valley. So, Harvey was proud to see his friends supporting him.

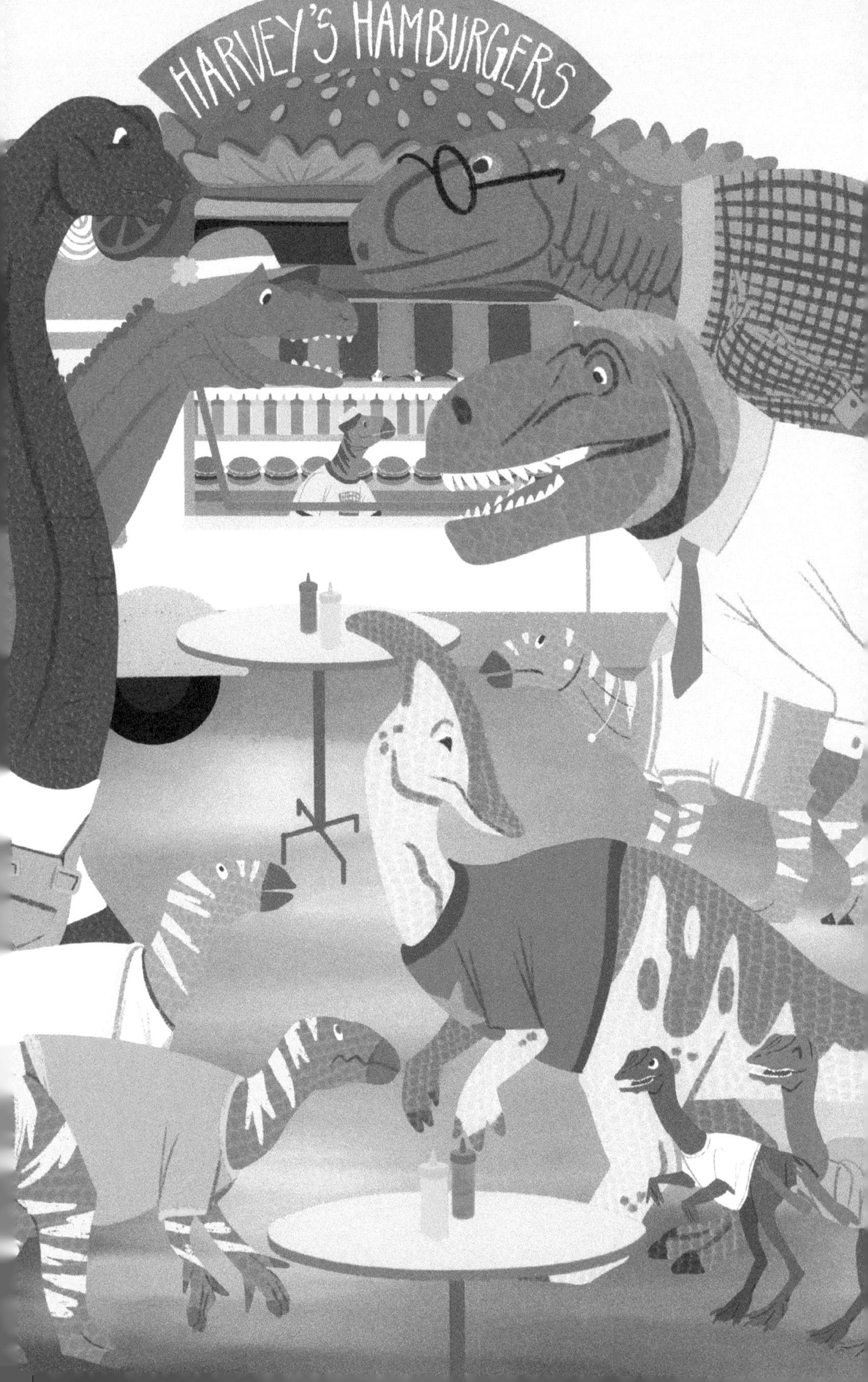
HARVEY'S HAMBURGERS

As Harvey's truck became more popular with the omnivores and herbivores, he expanded the menu to include salads and lettuce-wrapped hamburgers. The new foods drew in even more dinosaurs, and soon you could see Brachiosauruses, an Ankylosaur, and even a Styracosaurus or two joining the line.

38

One day, his family stepped up to the window to place their order. As Harvey cooked, they talked to him.

"We're sorry for not believing in you, Harvey. We can see now that you are very brave, and you have built a wonderful food truck business. We are very proud of you."

That night as Harvey went to bed, he dreamed of new foods to add to his menu. He woke up the next day with a smile and began to prepare his food truck. He was open for business!

40